Greetings,
People of Earth!

It's me, Carly! Ready for another exciting adventure, iCarly-style? Well, get ready because this one is a doozy!

Have you ever had your entire life flash before your eyes? That's exactly what happened to me when I was almost hit by a taco truck. Ugh, what an embarrassing way to die that would have been! But I wasn't too surprised that some of my favorite memories were making iCarly with my best friends, Sam and Freddie. Of course, I really didn't need a near-death experience to figure that out. So, grab a plate of Sam's special ribs and get ready for a super-juicy story—just be sure not to choke on your snacks while laughing . . . just ask Sam, it can happen!

And when you are done reading, tune in for the latest episode of iCarly—it wouldn't be the same without you! Bye for now! :)

Carly

People of Earth — don't miss a single
iCarly book!

iSaved Your Life!

iSaved Your Life!

Adapted by Aaron Rosenberg

Part 1: Based on "iSaved Your Life"
Written by Peter Tibbals & Eric Goldberg

Part 2: Based on "iTwins,"
Written by Peter Tibbals & Eric Goldberg

Based on the TV series *iCarly*
Created by Dan Schneider

SCHOLASTIC INC.

New York   Toronto   London   Auckland
Sydney   Mexico City   New Delhi   Hong Kong

If you purchased this book without a cover, you should be aware that this book is stolen property. It was reported as "unsold and destroyed" to the publisher, and neither the author nor the publisher has received any payment for this "stripped book."

No part of this work may be reproduced, stored in a retrieval system, or transmitted in any form or by any means, electronic, mechanical, photocopying, recording, or otherwise, without written permission of the publisher. For information regarding permission, write to Scholastic Inc., Attention: Permissions Department, 557 Broadway, New York, NY 10012.

ISBN 978-0-545-28406-6

© 2010 Viacom Inc. All Rights Reserved.
Nickelodeon, *iCarly*, and all related titles, logos, and characters are trademarks of Viacom International Inc.

Published by Scholastic Inc.
SCHOLASTIC and associated logos are trademarks and/or registered trademarks of Scholastic Inc.

12 11 10 9 8 7 6 5 4 3 2 1   10 11 12 13 14 15/0

Printed in the U.S.A. 40
First printing, September 2010

PART 1

¡Saved Your Life!

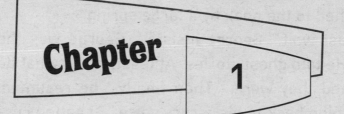

Chapter 1

The lights were dim. Ominous music could be heard rumbling in the background. Two shivering girls huddled near each other, crouched on the floor. A strange apparition hovered above them. A deep, chilling voice spoke:

". . . and when the rinse cycle began, the washing machine started to wobble and make *straaange* rumbling noises . . ."

Carly and Sam both glared at the piece of pink cloth floating above and between them. It was shaped and curved and satiny. It was, in fact, a bra.

"Okay, this 'ghost story' is going nowhere," Sam proclaimed. She was perched on a toy inchworm and had an Indian headdress over her long blond hair.

"You're not scary!" Carly agreed. She was sitting on an inchworm as well, but atop her long dark hair was a small helmet with a troll head attached to the peak by a large spring.

"Just wait," George insisted. George was the bra. He told ghost stories. At least, that's what he claimed they were. "Then finally," he resumed, switching back to his "scary voice," "I called customer service." He paused. "And they told me . . . my washing machine was out of warranty! *Aaaaah! Eeeeeee! Ooooooh!*" George fluttered about.

Sam rolled her eyes. "Anything else?" She was clearly not impressed.

George hesitated for a second. When the bra spoke again, it was in a quieter voice. "Can I come wash some clothes at your house?" he asked.

"No!" Sam punched the floating bra and he went spinning away.

"Get out of here, ya bra!" Carly insisted, slapping George away when he floated back within range.

"Hey!" George spun away again, drifting toward the back wall and out of view as Carly and Sam stood up and took off their headgear. The lights came back up as they did so. Freddie adjusted the video camera to accommodate the change in lighting.

Because, of course, they were filming.

Where else would anyone see a ghost-story-telling bra but on the Web show *iCarly*?

That was part of the fun of their show: You never knew what you might see next.

That skit only worked, however, if Carly and Sam took it seriously. Which they had. Hopefully the viewers had enjoyed it. They'd find out later, when they logged onto the *iCarly* Website and checked the comments.

Now, however, it was time to move the show along to the next segment.

"Okay," Carly announced, "a lotta you guys have emailed and texted us, asking if we'd—"

"Whoa!" Sam suddenly screamed and threw herself forward. She landed on a beanbag and hunched down into it. At the same time, she pulled a strange contraption from her belt and raised it to her lips. It looked like a cross between a small water pistol and a bendy straw.

Freddie backed up, startled and wary. Most of the time when Sam leaped forward it was to punch him. But this time she stayed down, focused on the door behind him.

"What?" Carly demanded. She wasn't as worried about her own safety — Sam never attacked her. That sort of violence was usually reserved for Freddie. Or random strangers. Or food.

"I thought I heard Spencer coming," Sam said over her shoulder. She didn't leave the protection of the beanbag.

Carly laughed and shook her head. "He's night fishing with Socko," she assured her best friend and co-host.

"Okay." Sam finally got up and rejoined Carly in the center of the studio.

"Sorry," Carly told her viewers. "Sam and Spencer are involved in a little game this week."

"It's called 'Assassin,'" Sam corrected her, raising the contraption toward the camera, "and it's not a game."

Carly laughed. "They use blowtubes with little paint balls and try to get each other." She pointed at Sam's device.

Sam scowled, trying to look fierce. "It's serious chiz." Then she broke into a grin. "Carly lost on the first day."

"Spencer whacked me while I was eating

4

toast," Carly agreed. She couldn't even be upset about her own brother taking her out like that. It had been pretty funny!

Besides, it wasn't as embarrassing as—

"And I got Freddie while he was doin' a camera test," Sam announced to the entire world. She jumped up and down. Carly joined her. "Show 'em, Fredbag!" They both spun around to watch the plasma screen set against the far wall.

Freddie sighed and hit a button on his laptop. The plasma screen swiveled out and played the clip. It was Freddie, standing in the studio, staring intently into the camera.

"Tilt it down?" Carly asked. For once she was off-camera and Freddie was on-screen. Usually he operated all of the equipment while Carly and Sam did the performing.

"Yeah," Freddie agreed. The camera angle tilted. "Wait, not that much. Back up."

"'Kay . . . like this?" The camera swiveled back up slightly.

Freddie nodded, but he was still frowning a little. "Yeah, but—"

Suddenly, a crazed shout came from some-

where off-camera. Freddie glanced up and his eyes widened.

"No, Sam," he pleaded, starting to raise his own blowtube. "Not now! Wait!"

Too late.

A large orange splatter suddenly burst across his chest, and Freddie toppled backward from the force of the impact.

The real Freddie stopped the clip and returned them to the live Web show, where Sam was crowing about her victory.

"I blow, I score!" She exulted. "Ninja!"

"So the only two people left in the game now are Sam and my brother, Spencer," Carly said.

"Not for long," Sam insisted. She leaned in close to the camera, raising her blowtube to her face and aiming it at the camera, gangsta style. "Spencer gonna get got."

Carly gave Sam one of her "you're a complete nutball" looks. "I apologize for her grammar," she told the camera, but the half-smile said she didn't really mean it.

Not that Sam was concerned. "I'm not educated," she admitted with a grin, "but I'm a lot of fun!"

Carly wrapped an arm around Sam's neck and proceeded to give her a noogie. "It's true!"

"Now," Sam announced, "to close the show . . ." She raised her blowtube and pointed it — right at the camera!

"No, Sam, don't!" Freddie begged.

Too late again.

Splat! Green paint struck the camera lens dead center.

Freddie growled at her. "And we're not clear!" But he shut it down anyway.

The end of another successful episode!

"I think that went well," Carly said as the three friends headed downstairs to the rest of her apartment. "Don't you?"

"Absolutely!" Sam agreed.

"Easy for you to say," Freddie complained as he followed the two girls into the loft elevator. "You're not the ones who have to clean the lens!"

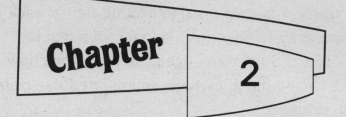

Chapter 2

The next morning, Carly traipsed downstairs to the kitchen and living room. She was dressed — in a hot-pink bunny suit!

She had almost reached the last step when her brother, Spencer, jumped up from behind the kitchen counter. He had a blowtube to his lips and shouted as he blew into it. Carly shrieked and covered her face with her arms just as a glob of orange paint struck the wall right in front of her.

She glared at the paint, then at her brother. How was it that Spencer was supposed to be the adult around here?

He had the decency to look embarrassed. "I thought you were gonna be Sam!" he explained.

That was it, Carly decided. She'd had enough. "Gimme it!" she ordered as she crossed to the kitchen. Even in the pink bunny suit she looked fierce.

But her brother wasn't going to cave that easily. "No, I need it!" he insisted.

She held out her hand. "Give. Me. IT!" The last word came out as a growl.

Spencer handed it over. "Now how am I gonna defend myself," he asked, "when Sam comes —"

Mentioning her name acted like a summons, because at that exact second Sam burst onto the upstairs landing. She charged down the stairs, screaming like a crazed monkey. She reached the last few steps with a leap and raised the blowtube. But Spencer had already dived behind the kitchen counter for safety.

And Sam found a large pink bunny blocking her path.

"Stop it!" Carly shouted. "Stop it!"

"But —" Her friend tried to argue.

Carly wasn't listening. "Give me your blowtube!" she shouted.

Sam scowled. "But all I wanna do —"

Carly cut her off with an *"Ehh!"* and a raised finger.

"Please —" Sam tried again.

Carly interrupted her with random sounds

again. "Ah ba ba ba!" Actually arguing with Sam rarely worked. Throwing noise at her and not letting her talk, however — that sometimes did the trick.

And it worked this time. Sam glowered and handed Carly her blowtube.

"You stand up," Carly called into the kitchen. Spencer's head popped up behind the counter a second later.

Carly was already walking toward the living room. "Now, I'm putting your guys' little Assassin game on hold til we finish shooting this dare for *iCarly*," she announced. "Are we clear?"

Both Sam and Spencer started to argue with her. *Honestly*, Carly thought, *it's like dealing with small children!*

"Are we clear?" she repeated, more loudly.

Both her brother and her friend sighed. "Yes'm. Okay."

Pleased with herself, Carly dropped both blowtubes on the couch. Luckily, they didn't go off.

"So," Spencer asked as he settled onto a kitchen stool, "what dare?" He was much more relaxed now that his rival had been disarmed.

Sam laughed. "A fan dared Carly to wear a bunny suit and offer to brush people's teeth for a dollar."

Spencer shook his head. "Man. Your Web show's weird." And coming from him, that was a compliment!

There was a knock at their loft's door. It wasn't locked, and a second later Freddie stepped in. He was wearing his jacket, his backpack, and a full camera rig. His trusty camcorder was already in his hand.

"Who's not ready?" he asked.

Sam grinned. "Let's do it." She swept her arms around, airplane style, and zoomed toward the door.

"We'll be back in two hours," Carly assured her brother as she followed Freddie out.

"Okay. Be careful!" Spencer replied. All three called out good-byes as they left, Sam bringing up the rear.

Spencer hopped off the stool and headed for the fridge. He was just reaching for the door handle when something slammed into the freezer by his head.

"Aaah!" He shrank back, staring at the green paint burst against the brushed steel surface. Then he turned, crouching a little as he tried to figure out what had just happened.

It was immediately obvious, however. Sam was back in the apartment, grinning. And in her hand she had—

Just then Carly burst back in. She rushed up next to Sam and snatched the thing from her hand. It was another blowtube, but half the size of the original.

"Where'd you get a little one?" Carly demanded.

Sam shrugged. "A good assassin always has a backup."

Carly shook her head. These two were impossible! "Up against the wall!" she ordered.

Sam didn't look too happy about that, but she complied. She knew the drill, and automatically put her hands on the bookshelf that held Spencer's paint cans. Carly followed her friend over there and kicked at her feet, doing her best impression of a movie prison guard.

"Feet apart," she instructed.

"Yeah!" Spencer shouted from safety, back in the kitchen. "Feet apart!"

Carly started patting Sam down. Sam's jeans had flared cuffs that were pulled down over her sneakers. But the right side bulged out a bit.

Carly lifted the cuff, exposing Sam's high-top sneaker, sock — and a second mini-blowtube tucked into them.

"Really?" she asked as she confiscated the toy weapon.

"Really?" her brother repeated.

Carly tossed both of the mini-blowtubes onto the couch. "Let's go," she told Sam, and swatted her on the butt to get her moving. They left again, and this time Carly shut the door behind her.

Spencer shook his head and studied the paint splotch on the freezer door. He tested it with his index finger. Still wet. Then, because he couldn't help it, he touched his finger to the tip of his tongue.

Yes, it was definitely paint.

"Oh, she's a clever one," he muttered, glaring at the front door.

But so was he.

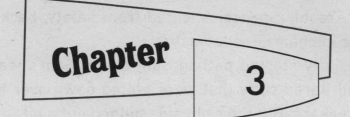

Chapter 3

It was later that same afternoon. Carly and Sam hadn't returned yet, and Spencer had decided to enjoy the Assassin-free zone by making himself a pizza. He actually liked cooking when he got the chance — it was just another type of art, really. But one you could eat!

He'd let the pizza cook long enough, he decided as he headed back into the kitchen. Time to see how it had turned out!

He pulled on a pair of potholders. "Okay, my pizza — the time has come!"

Crouching down, Spencer pulled open the oven door. It certainly smelled done!

"Oh, yes," he crooned. He reached in with both hands and carefully drew out the piping-hot disk. Then he stood, still clutching his prize. He sniffed. Oh, it smelled so good!

"Who's a pretty pie?" he asked his food as he

kicked the oven door shut again. It really was an impressive specimen! "Who's a—"

Just then the loft door swung open and Sam burst in. "Spencer!" she shouted. She had something small and yellow clutched in one hand.

"Hey!" Spencer cowered, dropping the pizza tray but holding the pizza itself in front of him like a shield. If there was anything Sam wouldn't want to damage, it was food.

Not that damaging it meant she wouldn't eat it, of course.

"Carly said the game is on hold until—" he reminded Sam as she rushed over to him.

"Freddie's hurt!" she interrupted.

"Yeah, right." Spencer smirked from behind his pizza shield. "I'm not fallin' for—"

Then Sam did the unthinkable. She tore the pizza from his grasp—and threw it to the ground! "I'm not kidding!" she insisted. "Freddie's hurt!"

Spencer straightened up. He'd never seen Sam discard food before. This must be serious!

"Wait, what happened?" he asked.

Sam tried to catch her breath. She looked really upset. Then it all came out in a rush. "Carly

15

was crossing the street and a big taco truck came around the corner and Carly didn't see the truck and so Freddie ran out and pushed Carly outta the way and—"

Sam ran out of steam a little bit at that point, which gave Spencer the chance to ask the question that was eating at him. "Is Carly okay?" If anything had happened to his little sister—

Fortunately, Sam nodded. "Yes! She's fine." Spencer discovered he could breathe again. "But Freddie got hit!"

Spencer pulled the potholders off his hands. "Okay, okay! Did you call nine-one-one—"

Sam said, "Yeah! Me and Carly both did!" She seemed to be calming down a little now. Spencer understood that. She'd told an adult, which meant she could let someone else take care of it from here on in.

Unfortunately for him, he was the adult!

He set the potholders down on the kitchen table, thinking. What needed to be done? Then he realized. "Oh, man. I better call Mrs. Benson at work!" Freddie's mom was overprotective

of Freddie to begin with. He could only imagine how she'd react when she heard about this!

He knew he didn't have a choice, though. He had to let her know. It was the right thing to do.

Spencer grabbed his phone and started dialing. He was still typing in Mrs. Benson's work number when he turned around — and realized that Sam was unwrapping the yellow thing she'd been carrying.

He paused. "You bought a taco?"

Sam nodded. "Uh-huh."

Spencer frowned down at her. "From the truck that hit Freddie?"

Sam groaned. "Well, me starving's not gonna help him!" Then she took a big bite.

Spencer just shook his head. Kids today!

As he dialed the phone, his eyes went to his pizza, still on the kitchen floor. He tried to remember the last time he'd mopped that floor. Maybe he could wipe it off?

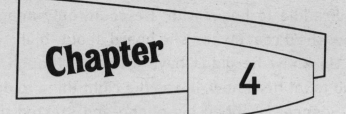

Chapter 4

"There, dear," Mrs. Benson cooed. "Let's get you all nice and cozy!" She fussed about, adjusting the covers for the thousandth time.

Freddie was used to his mom pampering him — and smothering him. Being injured only made it that much harder to resist.

And he was definitely injured. He'd broken his left leg in two places and had a hairline fracture in his right forearm. There were various cuts and bruises as well, but those weren't too severe. It was the two casts that made things difficult.

His mom had just stepped back, satisfied with her bed-tucking handiwork, when their apartment's front door security system chimed.

Mrs. Benson threw up her hands. "Oh, who is that?"

She went over to Freddie's bedroom door and the security panel set beside it. Activating the panel caused a picture to appear on the small screen. It was Spencer and Carly at the door.

Mrs. Benson activated the intercom. "Uch, what do you two want?" she asked.

"Can we please see Freddie?" Carly asked. It looked like she was holding flowers.

Mrs. Benson sighed, but punched in the security code. It took a minute — the code was actually forty-two digits long!

A small beep indicated that the system had accepted her password.

"Leave your shoes in the hall!" she instructed.

"Please be nice," Freddie urged.

A few seconds later, the door to his room swung open. "Hello," Spencer said as he stepped in.

Carly was right behind him. "Hey, Mrs. Benson," she told Freddie's mom. Mrs. Benson pointedly refused to look at her. "How is he?"

Now Mrs. Benson did look at her, but only to glare meaningfully. "Broken," she replied. "Damaged." She grimaced. "But I see you look fine, isn't that nice?"

Freddie rolled his eyes. "Mom —" he warned.

"And I see you brought flowers," Mrs. Benson

continued, "which will only exacerbate Freddie's allergies."

Freddie sighed. "Mom, I'm not allergic to flowers," he reminded her. He wasn't allergic to most of the things she thought he was.

As usual, mere logic didn't work on his mom. "And you weren't allergic to Mexican food trucks," she pointed out, "but look at you now!" She was practically in tears, and as usual Freddie found it impossible to stay mad at her.

"I'll just take these flowers," Mrs. Benson announced, snatching them out of Carly's hands. "And I'll soak them in bleach." She stormed out of the bedroom and down the hall.

"She's pretty upset," Freddie explained.

"No, really?" both Carly and Spencer replied.

"How ya doin'?" Spencer asked.

Freddie shrugged, and wished he hadn't. "Okay. Pretty sore."

Carly shook her head. "Sore? You have a broken leg and your arm is all smushed and it's all my fault —"

"It's not your fault," Freddie interrupted her.

"It is," Carly insisted. "If I'd seen that stupid

truck coming you never would have had to —"

Freddie tried again. "Stop." He knew she'd been blaming herself since it had happened.

Spencer provided a distraction, as always. "Hey, look," he announced, pointing at Freddie's cast, "his toes stick out of his cast." Spencer bent over and started messing with Freddie's toes. "This little piggy went to market," Spencer sang, tugging Freddie's middle toe, "and this little piggy got hit by a truck —"

That got Carly's attention. "Spencer!" she snapped. Her brother stopped and stood up immediately. It always amused Freddie how Carly was so much more adult than Spencer. Then again, there were times when Freddie felt like the adult compared to his mom, too.

"So, are you in much pain?" Spencer asked.

Freddie shook his head. "I was, but the doctor sent over some pills."

"You took one?" Carly was in full "mom" mode!

"Sorta," Freddie admitted. "My mom thinks I'll choke on pills so she pounds 'em with a mallet and puts the pill powder in my fruit sauce."

Spencer looked confused. "Fruit sauce?"

Freddie sighed. "My mom thinks I'll choke on fruit so she pounds it with a mallet—"

Spencer cut him off. "It's not my business." Then he looked around. "Can I use your bathroom?"

Freddie nodded. "Sure, right through there." He gestured toward the bathroom door.

"Thanks." Spencer left the room. Which left Freddie alone with Carly.

As always, Freddie couldn't help but notice how pretty she looked. He'd been smitten since the first time he'd met her, back when they were in sixth grade. And Carly had only gotten prettier as they'd gotten older. Right now she was looking a little uncertain about herself, and she was giving him a sweet little half-smile. The same one that always wowed her viewers. It worked just as well on Freddie, even after all this time.

She stepped closer. Then she tickled his toes, too—she just couldn't help herself. But Freddie smiled when she did it.

"You saved my life," Carly told him.

Freddie snorted. "C'mon."

Carly wouldn't let it go. "Sam said that truck would have run right over me."

Freddie paused to think about it. "Maybe," he admitted after a second. He was a little proud. He hadn't even thought about it at the time — he'd just seen the truck, seen Carly in its path, and leaped in to push her to safety.

Then the truck had hit him.

After that, he hadn't been thinking much of anything beyond "Oh man, that hurt!"

But now he was able to look back and realize that maybe it had been kind of brave after all.

Carly was still smiling at him, a soft, sweet smile. Neither of them was saying anything. It was a real Hallmark moment.

So of course Sam had to ruin it.

"Hey, you guys in here?" she shouted from out in the hall.

"Yeah, we're in Freddie's room," Carly replied, turning toward the door.

Then Spencer emerged from the bathroom, looking around wildly. "Did I hear Sam?" he demanded. He had his blowtube in his hand.

"Yeah," Freddie replied, "she's —"

He didn't even get a chance to finish.

"*Aaah!*" Spencer shouted. He spun toward the

door, raised the blowtube to his lips, and exhaled sharply. The paintball shot out and whizzed through the open door.

There was a splat, and a scream.

Not a Sam-scream.

A second later, Mrs. Benson walked back into Freddie's room. She looked completely shocked and horrified. A large splash of bright orange paint decorated her neck and chest, right above her V-neck sweater. She was carrying a wilted, pale collection of stems and leaves.

"Ah, I'm sorry," Spencer started. "I didn't —"

But Carly interrupted him. "What happened to the flowers?" she asked. She'd just realized that those were the same bouquet she'd brought for Freddie.

Mrs. Benson glared at her. "I soaked them in bleach and pounded them with a mallet."

Carly wondered if that meant Mrs. Benson was going to try to feed the flowers to Freddie, along with his fruit sauce.

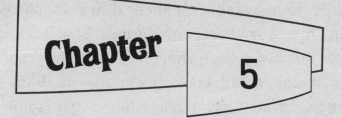

Chapter 5

Sam was walking to her locker the next day. She glanced from side to side as she walked, ready for anything.

Anything except the hand that reached out from behind to tap her on the shoulder. "Hey, Sam!" someone said from close-by.

Too close.

Sam spun around, drawing her blowtube and bringing it to her lips in one swift motion.

The person behind her screamed and cowered. "Don't! I'm just a Gibby!"

She straightened and lowered the blowtube.

"Sorry," she told him. "I'm on the lookout for Spencer. We're the only two left in the game." She couldn't believe Carly's brother hadn't mounted an attack yet.

Gibby looked confused. "But you're at school," he pointed out. Gibby was sweet, but a little naïve.

"So?" Sam asked. "Spencer'll try to sneak up on me anywhere, anytime." She looked around quickly. "Even here." Then she realized that she could take advantage of Gibby's presence. "Watch my back while I get somethin' outta my locker," she ordered. She turned back toward her locker, and Gibby followed after her.

"And what if I see Spencer?" Gibby asked.

Sam spun back around to face him. "Use your face and body to protect me." *Duh!* Did she really have to explain that?

Gibby smiled. "Ah, like a human shield."

"I was gonna say bullet-monkey," Sam admitted, "but whatever tickles your peach."

She opened her locker. Gibby put his back to her and blocked her from view. Gibby was taller and wider than she was, so he provided excellent coverage.

She was just grabbing her Algebra textbook when Gibby stiffened behind her.

"There's Spencer!" he shouted, pointing. "With a fake beard!"

Sam whipped around. Sure enough, a tall,

bearded man in a dark suit had just come down the stairs. Sam snarled. What a weak disguise! She dropped to one knee, squinted down the length of her blowtube, targeted him, and blew hard. The paintball nailed the bearded man, splattering him right over his suit's chest pocket. He looked shocked.

"Oy!" he shouted. Oy? That didn't sound like Spencer!

Mr. Stern came running down the stairs. He looked horrified. "Rabbi Goldman?" he said as he reached the bearded man.

She turned on Gibby, who was standing right behind her. "That was a real rabbi!" she shouted in his face.

"I didn't know!" Gibby yelped. "I don't have cable!"

Mr. Stern stomped over to Sam. "Puckett," he snapped, "you just earned yourself triple detention!" Then he walked away. "Come along, Rabbi." Mr. Stern took the rabbi by the arm and led him toward the front door.

Sam turned to glare at Gibby. He gulped. He knew better than to mess with her — and he'd just

gotten her triple detention! He was a dead man.

She raised her blowtube slowly. Gibby sighed. He didn't bother to hide. In fact, he straightened up. If he was going to take it, he'd take it like a man.

Sam put the blowtube to her mouth. Gibby looked away. No one should see their own doom like that, up close and personal.

Instead he ran a finger along his left temple, making sure his hair was properly in place. Best to go out looking his best.

"How's my hair look, Sam?" he asked softly.

Sam gave him a small nod. "You look good, Gib." She kept her voice low, too. Out of respect.

They stood there a second, two friends knowing what had to be done to put things right. Then Sam fired. *Spat!* The paintball struck Gibby right in the center of his forehead. Sam walked away without another word. Gibby stood there, looking up as if he could see the purple paint dripping down his face.

He couldn't fault her for it. Given his betrayal, it was a fair price to pay.

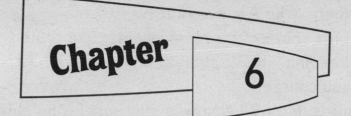

Chapter 6

That night, Carly stopped by Freddie's apartment again. It helped that they literally lived across the hall from each other! This time she didn't bring flowers, however. She tried cupcakes instead.

"Thanks for letting me in, Mrs. Benson," she told Freddie's mom as they walked down the hall to Freddie's room. Carly held the tray of cupcakes carefully. She'd spent too much time baking and decorating them to let Freddie's mom pound them with a mallet!

"*Hmph,*" was the only reply she got. Freddie's mom was wearing a coat and carrying her handbag, which was odd, even for her. Where was she going?

Carly walked into Freddie's room with a big smile, holding out the tray to impress him with her baking skills — and he wasn't there. The bed was empty.

"Where is he?" she asked.

"In the shower," his mom replied. She couldn't resist adding, "His first cleansing since the accident you caused."

Clearly, Mrs. Benson was still upset. And still mad at her. But she was speaking to Carly, which was an improvement.

Carly tried yet again to apologize. "Mrs. Benson —" she began.

But Freddie's mom cut her off, shoving her hand in Carly's face to stop her cold. "I have to go to the pharmacy and get his meds," she announced. She turned toward the bathroom door. Now Carly could hear the sounds of the shower. She wondered how Freddie managed to keep his casts from getting wet. Wouldn't that ruin them?

"Freddie," Mrs. Benson yelled, "I'll be back in thirty-six minutes!" She brushed past Carly and paused. "It should have been you," Mrs. Benson whispered in Carly's ear. Then she stomped out of the room. A minute later, Carly heard the front door slam.

Great. Carly and Mrs. Benson had never exactly been friends — Freddie's mom felt Carly was a bad influence on Freddie, giving him ideas like going outside and having friends and eating solid foods — but they'd always had an uneasy truce before. Now Mrs. Benson hated her.

And Carly had to admit, she had reason for it. It was Carly's fault Freddie had gotten hurt, after all.

Carly had been thinking about that a lot since the accident. About how it was her fault — and about how Freddie had risked his life for her. How brave he'd been. And how sweet.

Gosh, that shower was taking a long time!

Bored, she set the cupcakes down on a table and started poking around his room. There was one of the little computerized games Freddie liked — she picked it up and fiddled with it for a second before setting it back down. She wandered over to his dresser and admired a little Army man standing there. Two more were perched atop a small box — maybe a music box, but Carly didn't dare open it to find out. She smiled and wandered toward the set of computers on Freddie's desk.

Then she heard a loud thud from the bathroom.

Carly rushed over to the bathroom and skidded to a stop just outside the partially open door. "Freddie?"

"Mom?"

"No, it's Carly!" she shouted back. "Your mom left! What happened?"

"I fell!" he answered.

Oh, no! "Are you okay?" Carly realized she was starting to hyperventilate. She forced herself to calm down.

"Yeah," Freddie replied, which certainly helped her relax. "But, ah, I don't think I can get up."

Right, Carly thought. *Because of the casts. That cover the injuries. The ones he got because of me.*

"All right," she decided out loud. "I'll come help you!"

"NO!!!" Freddie shouted as she took a step. "Don't come in here!"

That made her pause. "Why not?"

"Cuz!" There was a pause. "I'm . . . in the shower."

Oh. Oh! Carly blushed. Right! No, rushing into the bathroom right now would be a bad idea!

32

Still, she had to do something! "Well, you can't just lay there on the shower floor for thirty-six minutes!" she pointed out. Then she had an idea. What if she couldn't see him? "Um, just a sec!" she told Freddie.

She glanced around his room. There had to be something — yes! Sitting on his dresser were goggles! Carly rushed over and grabbed them. Perfect! Now she just needed something — she pulled open the top dresser drawer and grabbed the first piece of clothing she found.

Then she shrieked. She was holding a pair of Freddie's underwear! She dropped them back into the drawer and slammed it shut, trying to scrub the image from her mind. Then she tried the drawer beside that one. Socks. Much better!

"Hang on!" she called.

Carly pulled out two socks and shoved one into each goggle. Then she stuck the goggles on her head and tugged them down over her eyes. Perfect! She couldn't see a thing with the socks there!

"All right, Freddie!" she shouted, turning

and feeling her way back toward the bathroom. "I can't see anything! I'm coming in!"

She stepped carefully into the bathroom. She could tell she'd cleared the door — since she had left her shoes out in the hall, she could feel the difference between Freddie's wooden floor and the bathroom's cold tiles. She edged along carefully — the last thing she needed was to fall down herself. Or, worse, to land on Freddie.

"Where are you?" she called out. She didn't have to shout anymore, at least.

"Down here," Freddie answered. "Can you turn off the water?"

"Uhhh . . ." She found the shower curtain and used that to feel her way to the far wall. The water was much louder right here and she could feel the shower spray on her face. That meant the nozzle was right in front of her. And the knobs should be right about — here! Her hands found the metal knobs. "Yeah, here." She gave them a hard twist and the water slowed and then stopped, though not before Carly got soaked along that side.

"All right," she said. She crouched down and came in contact with something that crinkled.

It felt like plastic. Then she realized—it was a plastic bag! Freddie had wrapped his cast so he could take a shower! He was so smart! And if his leg was *here*, that meant he was lying *this* way. After what seemed like the weirdest game of hide-and-seek, Carly finally "found" Freddie and helped him up.

"Um, put your arm around my shoulder," she instructed, ducking her head to help him.

"Okay." Freddie shifted and put his arm around her. "Ow, ow, easy," he warned as she started to straighten up again.

"Can you move your leg?" she asked him.

"Sorta." She felt it brush against her side. *"Owww."* But his weight had shifted, and she was able to stand up a bit more now.

"Don't slip," she warned as she stood up completely. If he did, they'd both go down! "Just hold onto my arm."

"I got it," Freddie assured her. She heard the plastic bag scrape against the floor and knew he was standing up, too. It was working!

Now she just had to help him out of the bathroom and back to his bed.

"Easy," Carly urged, turning and finding the bathroom wall with her free hand. She started guiding them back out of the room. "Just move slow."

"Wait," Freddie said after a second. "Let me get my robe."

Carly tried not to giggle. "Okay." Yes, a robe would be a good thing!

She felt Freddie twist and stretch, then there was something long and billowy brushing against her hand. The robe! She grasped at it and found a sleeve, which she held out.

"Stick your arm through here," she said.

"Okay, okay." She could feel him shifting, and then his arm was in the robe.

"You got it?" She figured he could handle the rest himself!

"Yep." A bit of rustling, and his arm returned to her shoulder, but now it was dressed. That was a relief! She considered taking the goggles off now, but wasn't sure how well Freddie had managed with the robe. What if he was only partially robed? No, better to keep the goggles on and fumble around a bit more! Much safer.

She found the bathroom door and edged herself through it, turning sideways so Freddie would be able to get through after her without bumping his leg. Then it was down the step and across the room toward his bed. At least she hoped so.

"Are we walking the right way?" she asked after a minute. She didn't remember his room being this big!

"Yeah," Freddie assured her. "Just keep going." His voice sounded strained.

"Okay."

"*Oww,*" he said a second later.

"It hurts?" She felt a pang of guilt all over again.

"It doesn't feel good," he admitted. She could tell he was trying not make her feel any worse, which was sweet of him. But then he'd always been sweet. Especially to her.

"Where's the bed?" she asked. All she felt around her was empty air.

"Right here." Freddie was ahead of her slightly, and she could feel him stop as he bumped into something. Then her legs brushed it as well. Yes! They'd made it!

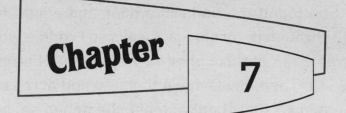

Chapter 7

"**O**kay," Carly said, feeling the rush of victory. Amazing how something as simple as walking across a room could be a challenge!

"Just lemme . . ." Freddie said. Carly felt his weight shift. "I'll sit first." His arm left her shoulder and the bed creaked as he sank onto it.

"Get under the covers," Carly ordered. She was eager to get rid of the goggles!

"Okay, I'm doin' it." She felt something brush her arm — the sheets, maybe? The mattress rustled.

"Ya got it?"

"Yeah," he replied after another minute. "Whew. Okay, you can take off the goggles."

She yanked them off her head and tossed them aside. Freddie lay under the covers, in the same place he'd been when she'd visited the other day. Except for the fact that his hair was still wet and

he was wearing different pajamas, she could have thought he hadn't even moved.

"That was scary," she admitted. She hugged herself, and grimaced as she felt how soaked her sleeve and shoulder were on the one side. "And wet."

"Yeah, thanks for helping me." Freddie smiled at her, and Carly felt something in her twitch. Why had she never noticed before what a cute smile he had?

Then she registered what he'd said, and frowned. "If it wasn't for me, you wouldn't need my help."

"Will you stop with that?" he asked her.

She looked at him for a minute. Had she ever really stopped to look at him before? He'd always just been Freddie. But maybe that wasn't his fault. Maybe it was hers.

"Y'know, everyone at school is saying you're a hero," she told him.

He actually chuckled at that. "I don't feel like a hero."

"Well, you are one." She smiled. "To me."

She stepped up to the bed and leaned in toward

him. He had such pretty eyes! How had she missed that all these years? He was staring up at her, and she could tell he was confused. *Maybe this will help*, she thought to herself.

Then she kissed him.

It was sweet and gentle. Just like Freddie.

They broke apart after a second, and Carly smiled. Freddie smiled back.

She kissed him again. This time they stayed together.

"Freddie," a voice announced behind them, "I got you some—"

Then Mrs. Benson screamed. Carly jumped back, startled and embarrassed. Caught kissing by his mom! Carly screamed, too. So did Freddie.

Mrs. Benson found her voice first.

"What the yuck?" she gasped.

"Nothing!" Carly insisted, jumping up.

"Mom, we were just—" Freddie started.

The two of them fell all over their words, trying to explain.

Finally, out of desperation, Carly almost shouted, "I was just taking his temperature! See?" She stuck her finger in Freddie's mouth, pulled

it out, and looked at it. "Ninety-eight point six!" she declared. "Healthy as a duck! Bye!" And she sprinted for the door.

"Carly, don't leave!" Freddie begged.

But Mrs. Benson had recovered from her shock. She grabbed the first thing at hand — a pair of Freddie's underwear — and began swatting Carly with it.

"She's beating me with your underwear!" Carly shouted. She ran. Behind her, she could hear the sound of a spray — no doubt Mrs. Benson was hosing Freddie down with something anti-bacterial. She just hoped it wasn't bleach.

Carly raced out of their apartment, slammed the door behind her, and leaned against it with a big sigh. What had just happened? What had she done? And did she want to do it again?

She was still trying to sort out her feelings when a figure leaped out of the bush in the corner of the hallway.

"Hey, Carls!" it shouted.

"*Aaah!*" Carly jumped. Then she realized the figure had long blond hair beneath its bush-covered helmet. It was Sam! She was wearing camouflage.

"You scared me!" Carly accused her best friend.

All Sam did was laugh at her. "Yeah, I saw that!"

"What were you doing behind that bush?"

"Lying in wait so I can get the drop on Spencer when he comes home." Sam held up her blowtube. Then she looked more closely at Carly. "Man, you look even whiter than usual. You okay?"

"Yeah, I'm fine," Carly responded. She didn't feel it, though!

Sam's next question was, "Freddie okay?"

"Yes!" Carly forced herself to laugh. "What are you, the girl of many questions?" She fumbled for her keys and unlocked her own door.

"Uh, what just happened in there?" Sam asked her.

Carly ignored her and pushed the door open. She closed it, but something made her yank the door open again.

"I kissed Freddie!" she shouted.

Then she ducked back inside and slammed the door shut.

Chapter 8

The next day, Freddie's doctors decided he was well enough to return to school.

Carly was waiting for him in the hallway. "Hi," she said. It was the first time they'd spoken since the kiss the other day.

"Hey," Freddie replied. He gave her a shy smile. He was so sweet!

Carly stepped closer and kissed him.

When they finally broke apart, Carly smiled at him. "Ready for school?"

"Absolutely." Together they headed down the hall.

Sam was waiting for them when they got there.

"Well, good morning, Mr. and Mrs. Benson," she announced as they reached her.

Carly and Freddie both rolled their eyes at her.

A bell rang through the halls.

"Oh, second bell," Carly said. She gave Freddie a quick kiss as she left. "See ya after class."

He smiled. "Yep."

"Yeah, savor it," Sam told him.

"Savor what?"

Sam gave him a mocking grin. "The love. The Carly love."

"What's your problem?" Freddie asked.

"Not my problem. Yours." Sam turned and walked away. Freddie hobbled after her.

"Wait," Freddie insisted.

"Go to class, Crutchie," Sam warned.

But Freddie didn't budge. "What problem do I have?"

Sam paused. "You want the truth?" she said finally.

Freddie nodded. "Let's hear it." He had courage, she'd give him that.

Sam sighed. "Remember two years ago when I dated that guy, Eric Mosby? With the big nose?"

"Sure, Noseby Mosby."

"Uh-huh." Sam frowned just thinking about it. "And remember how he tried to get me to be his girlfriend for like six months, and I kept sayin' 'Get away from me or I'll kill you' — and then he

44

bought me a subscription to the Bacons-of-the-World Club? And then, boom, I thought I was in love with the guy?"

Sam could tell by Freddie's expression that he didn't get what she was saying. "I'm listening."

"I was never in love with him," Sam explained. "I was in love with the foreign bacon that kept showin' up at my door every month, like a beautiful, greasy dream."

She turned away and began dialing the combination to her locker.

Behind her, Freddie laughed. "Uh, I doubt that bacon could make you think you're in love with someone."

Sam spun around to face him. "You ever had Bolivian bacon?" she demanded. He shook his head. "It changes you." Just thinking about it made her feel all funny inside.

"Well, I didn't buy Carly any foreign bacon," Freddie pointed out. "I saved her life."

"And that's Carly's bacon," Sam insisted. "She's in love with what you did, not you."

"You just can't stand the idea of Carly and me

as a couple," he accused. But she could see that what she'd said had struck home.

Sam saw no reason to deny his charge. "Very true," she agreed. "It makes me wanna puke up blood. But still" — she looked him in the eye — "what I said is true . . . and you know it."

"I gotta get to class," was all Freddie said in reply. He hobbled off, but Sam could tell he was thinking about it. Good. She didn't want to see either of them get hurt, and being in a relationship for the wrong reason — that would hurt. A lot.

With a sigh she turned back to her locker and yanked it open — and stepped back, startled.

"*Heeeeeere's Spencer!*" Spencer shouted. He was inside her locker! He raised his blowtube and started cackling. "*Hahahhahaha —*"

Sam slammed the locker shut again, spun the lock closed, and walked away.

Behind her, she heard Spencer's voice, though the locker door muffled it. "I gotta quit saying witty things before I blow," he complained.

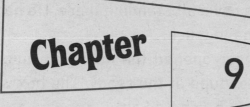

Chapter 9

The next day, Spencer was in the kitchen, washing some dishes.

Ding-dong!

At the sound of the doorbell, he dropped the plate in his hand and hunkered down, yanking his blowtube from its belt loop. Then he made his way across the living room, pausing only to grab a pillow and hold it in front of him like a shield.

At least it wasn't pizza this time.

"Hello?" he called out, making his voice high and creaky like a little old lady. "This is the housekeeper! I'm very old and not Spencer."

Ding-dong!

"Who is it?" Spencer demanded.

"Delivery for Spencer Shay," a man replied.

Spencer reached the front door and put one eye to the peephole. There was a man in a standard delivery service coverall standing there. He had a large box on a hand truck.

"Okay." Spencer opened the door and quickly leaned back, blowtube at the ready. The box was easily large enough to hold Sam.

"Hey," the guy said.

Spencer nodded. He kicked the box, listening closely, but he didn't hear any yelps from inside. Finally he nodded. "Okay. Bring it in."

He backed away quickly, then turned and leaped behind his bottle-bot, using it for cover as the delivery guy set the box down on the living room floor.

"And there ya go," the guy said.

"Wait. Open it up," Spencer ordered.

The delivery guy shrugged but did it.

Spencer squinted, trying to see into the box from his angle. "You see a girl in there?"

The deliveryman laughed. "No." Then he looked at Spencer. "Why, did you order one?"

"No!" Spencer came down to look in the box himself. "What's in it?"

"Uh . . ." the delivery guy peered in, rooting around through the packing peanuts that

filled the interior. "Just—" He smiled and straightened, pulling out an enormous lollipop. "This."

"Just a lollipop?" Spencer holstered his blow-tube and reached for the giant sweet.

"Yeah." The delivery guy started to offer it to him, then stopped. "But where I come from, we don't call it a lollipop."

Spencer frowned. "What do you call it?"

The delivery guy grinned at him. "A sucker!"

Spencer's eyes widened as he realized what the man had just said. He'd been had!

Before he could react, the delivery guy dove behind the couch. At the same time, Spencer saw a blur of motion from the open doorway.

It was Sam. She swung down from above the door and hung there, suspended, staring right at him.

Her blowtube was already in her hand.

"*Nooo!*" Spencer cried. He yanked on his own blowtube, wrestling it from its holster, and began to raise it.

But Sam had been ready. She brought her blowtube to her lips.

Spencer was still lifting his own weapon when Sam exhaled hard.

Splat!

A paintball slammed into him, hitting him square in the forehead.

Spencer flailed and fell backward, his blow-tube falling from his hand.

As he hit the floor, he caught a glimpse of Sam dropping down from her perch and landing on her feet.

Then she started crowing.

"Yeah, baby!" she shouted down at him, waving her arms about. "Momma wins! I am the ultimate assassin!" She started jumping about, screaming and hollering.

Spencer could do nothing but lie there, beaten and humiliated.

Then Sam spotted the giant lollipop. She stooped and scooped it up.

"You're not gonna eat this, are you?" she asked, waving it in Spencer's face. Right before she took a great big lick.

Slurp!

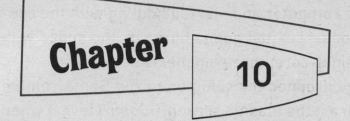
Diddle-diddle-dee, diddle-din-din-din!

Carly stared at the plasma screen in the *iCarly* studio. She was holding a toy violin. Her fingers flew on the strings, while she sawed the bow back and forth at lightning speed.

Rock Hero was hard!

She glanced behind her as the elevator opened and Freddie stepped out. He had some cables in one hand and some kind of computer gadget in the other, and he managed to hold onto them while he used his crutches to walk.

"There you are!" Carly said. She smiled.

"Here I am," Freddie agreed. "Spencer tell you I was comin' over?"

Carly nodded. "Yeah, he said you wanna fix something on the *iCarly* site?"

"Uh-huh." Freddie set the cables down on top

of the computer and started fiddling with the connections. "I'm just gonna bump up the speed with this eight-core, three gigahertz server."

She dropped the violin and used Sam's remote to retract the plasma screen. "*Oooh*, I love it when you talk all techie."

He seemed surprised by her statement. "Really?"

She nodded as she walked over to join him by the computer. "Yeah. It's cute and geeky at the same time." She grinned. "It's cu-ky."

That got him to laugh, but he still looked unsure. "You never called my tech-talk cu-ky before."

"Well"—she smiled at him—"that was before we were, y'know . . ."

Talking wasn't getting her anywhere, so Carly resorted to other methods. She stepped in close, put her arms around his neck, and kissed him.

She was completely surprised when, after a few seconds, he actually pulled away!

"You retreated," she said, studying him.

"I didn't retreat," Freddie argued. But Carly knew better.

"You kinda did," she insisted. "What's wrong?"

"Nothing." He looked down at the computer. "It's just, uhhh . . . so are we, like, boyfriend and girlfriend now?"

Carly blushed. "I dunno, maybe."

"Oh."

Carly frowned. "Well, don't say 'Oh' like that."

He chuckled and spread his arms wide. "I just said, 'Oh.'"

"No," she corrected him, "you said it like you were at a raffle, and you won a prize, and then you found out the prize was just a can of soup, so you go 'Oh.'" She made a long, funny face.

"You know I like you way better than most soups," Freddie assured her.

"Well, yay." They both laughed and Carly felt better. She made her way around the computer again. "Now, whaddaya wanna do — kiss, or bump up your four-score giggle-jam server?"

Freddie smiled. "Eight-core, three gigahertz."

"Yeah, that's really interesting," Carly said mockingly. "C'mere." She put her arms around his neck again and leaned in to kiss him once more.

For a second, everything was great. Then Freddie made a strange noise and broke away from her again. And this time he actually hobbled all the way across the room!

Carly stared at him. "Wow, you seriously don't wanna kiss me." She tried not to show how hurt she was by that. "Why?"

The thing was, Freddie was the one who looked like he was in pain. "Cuz," he replied. He hesitated. After a second he spit out, "I'm just bacon!"

"You're bacon?"

"Foreign bacon," he clarified.

Carly laughed. She couldn't help it. "Did that taco truck hit you in your brain?" she asked.

She moved a bit closer, and Freddie groaned and shook his head.

Carly was still confused. "I thought you've wanted me to be your girlfriend since the first day you met me," she said softly.

"I have," Freddie replied.

"Well? I'm standin' here with my lips all glossed up and you're treating me like I'm your icky cousin Amanda." That had come out a bit harsher than Carly had intended, but she was still feeling hurt. And puzzled. What was going on here?

"Amanda is disgusting," Freddie agreed.

iSaved Your Life

Filming an episode of *iCarly*.

Sam and I always have fun together!

Sam demonstrating the game Assassin!

I had to wear a bunny costume on a dare from an *iCarly* viewer!

Sam tells Spencer about Freddie's accident.

Freddie resting after he was hurt.

Spencer and I visit Freddie.

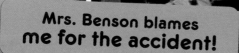
Mrs. Benson blames me for the accident!

Sam was hiding from Spencer during her game of Assassin!

Everyone at school is calling Freddie a hero!

Sam telling Freddie
that she thinks my feelings for him aren't real.

iTwins

Sam and I filming a new episode of *iCarly*.

Freddy doesn't believe Sam has a twin sister since we are always tricking him!

Me with Sam's twin sister, Melanie

Spencer is being bullied by Chuck, a boy who lives in our building.

Melanie likes Freddie!

Freddie tries to decide what to wear
on his date with Melanie!

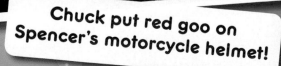

Chuck put red goo on
Spencer's motorcycle helmet!

Hanging out in the loft.

Even though they look alike, Sam and Melanie couldn't be more different!

"Freddie—" she started, but he cut her off.

"Okay," he said quickly, "you know how you've always said you like me, but that you don't like me 'that way'? Ya know, 'the good way'?" He waggled his eyebrows at her.

"Yeah," Carly argued, "but that was—"

"Before I saved your life."

She shrugged. "So?"

Freddie sighed. "Nothing's changed," he pointed out. "I'm still the same Freddie, and you're still the same Carly."

"But I love y—" Carly insisted. And again he didn't let her finish.

"You love what I did," he corrected. "You love that I risked my life to save yours. But I don't think you're in love with me." He shook his head. "You just think you are."

Carly walked away, thinking about that. Was he right? When had she started noticing him "that way"? It had been after he'd fallen in the shower—and after she'd heard everyone in school talking about what a hero he was. What if he was right? What if he was just, what had he called himself? Bacon?

Then something dawned on her. "You mean like when Sam dated Noseby Mosby because he got her all that —"

"— bacon," she and Freddie said together.

He nodded. "Yeah, exactly."

Carly looked down, away, anywhere but him. When she finally did look at him, it was all she could do not to cry. "So," she asked after a second, "you don't want me to be your girlfriend?"

"No, I do," he assured her. And she could see that he meant it. "But —" He took a deep breath. "I think we should wait a while. Til I'm outta this cast, and this whole hero thing wears off. And then" — he hobbled a few steps closer — "if you still wanna be my girlfriend, I'd be really psyched about it." The smile he gave her was so sweet it warmed her all over.

She couldn't be angry at him after that, or even hurt. After all, he hadn't rejected her. He just wanted to be sure she was really into him for himself, not for something he'd done.

And that was really noble of him. And really sweet.

"Okay," she agreed.

They both looked at each other. *What now?* Carly wondered. And she could tell he was thinking the same thing. When he'd stepped out of the elevator they'd been boyfriend and girlfriend. Now they weren't. But they'd been kissing just a minute ago. It was kind of hard to fall back into their usual banter after something like that.

"*Pffft,*" Freddie said, blowing air through his lips.

"*Pfffft,*" Carly agreed, doing the same.

They both laughed.

"I should probably get home," Freddie announced, "so my mom can spray me." He headed over to the elevator and pushed the button. The door rose immediately and he hauled himself inside.

Carly turned and followed him. "Well, I'll see you tomorrow," she promised. She wanted to make sure he knew she wasn't mad at him. And that they were still the best of friends.

"Yeah," he agreed. "Ummm. . . ." He looked away, then back at her. "Listen, when we kissed before, I didn't realize that would be our last one — for a while. So I was thinkin', maybe, if you wanted to . . ." His voice trailed off.

Carly smiled. Then she leaned in and gave him a kiss — on the cheek.

His answering smile was just as bright as if she'd given him the moon.

"Good night, Freddie," she told him softly as she stepped back out of the elevator. He nodded and let the elevator close.

The last thing Carly heard, as the elevator started down, was Freddie's anguished groan.

"What did I do?"

"You were honest with me," Carly whispered, though she knew there was no way he could hear her. "Because that's who you are. And that's why I'll always love you, whether it's as a friend . . . or as something more."

She glanced around the studio and spotted the violin where she'd dropped it. Snatching it up, she turned Rock Hero on again. After all that, beating some silly violin solo should be a piece of cake!

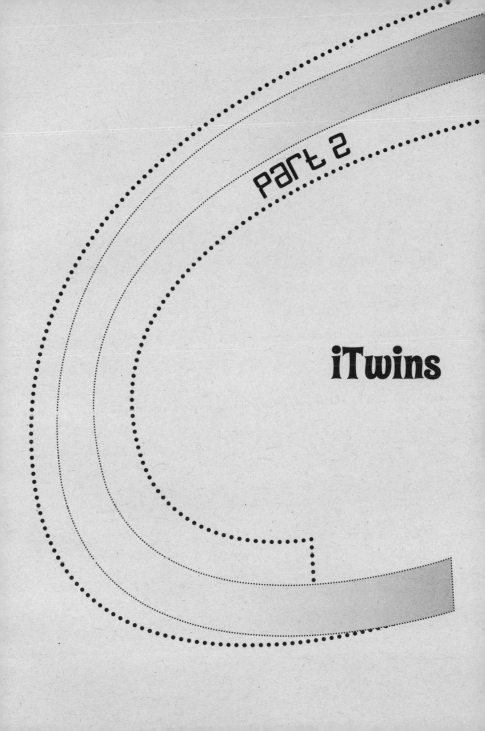

part 2

iTwins

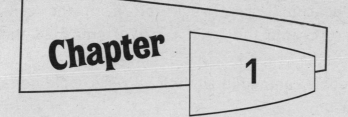

Chapter 1

*T*oot-toot!
Chug-a-chug-a-chug-a!

"Awww," Carly cooed. "Look at it!" She was on her knees, watching a little toy train.

"Cute little choo-choo," Sam agreed next to her, blond hair beside brunette. They stood by a small table that had been set up in the *iCarly* studio for the train. Freddie stood a short way away, his camera on his shoulder as usual. They were filming another *iCarly* episode.

"Go, little choo-choo train!" Carly told it.

"Woo-woo!" both girls shouted, tugging imaginary whistle cords.

They clambered to their feet.

Then Sam glanced up. "And here comes the big rock!" she announced, jumping up and down.

Carly pulled a rope beside her, and —
Wham!

A beachball-sized rock fell from the ceiling—right into the train table! It smashed the table to the ground, crushing it and the train!

Freddie zoomed in so their viewers could get a better look.

Then Carly spoke. "And that proves once again—" she said.

"—that big rock beats choo-choo train," Sam finished for her.

Carly shrugged and put her hands on her hips. "Hard to beat the big rock."

"It really is," Sam agreed.

"Okay!" Carly announced as she and Sam moved away from the devastation. "Next on *iCarly*—"

Sam took over. "—we're gonna show you a fun little video that we shot at school yesterday."

Freddie groaned. "Aw, great," he muttered.

Sam grinned into the camera. "I call this video, 'Gullible Freddie.' Check dis out."

The video appeared on Carly's big plasma screen.

It was the hall of their school. Then Freddie wandered into the picture. But he was wearing a

clown suit! He even had on a curly orange wig and a big red button nose!

Other students stared and laughed as he walked down the hall. The camera pulled back just as he reached the corner and turned — to see Sam and Carly at their lockers.

"Hey!" Freddie called to them. "Why aren't you guys dressed like clowns?"

The girls laughed and shut their lockers. "What do you mean?" Sam asked, walking around him to get a better view of his clown getup.

"I got an email from school," he told them, "saying that today was Clown Day. Wait —"

Then he groaned. The girls burst into giggles.

"You guys sent me that email," Freddie accused.

Carly pointed across him to Sam, who was on his other side. "She made me!"

Watching it, Freddie shook his head.

On-screen, clown-Freddie looked around — and spotted something. "Wait, is this on camera?" He charged toward the picture, a clown gone berserk. "Gibby, come here!"

"No!" They could hear Gibby screaming as the camera retreated. "Get away from me. No!"

The image vanished as clown-Freddie caught up with Gibby and took the camera away.

Back in the *iCarly* studio, the plasma screen retracted. Carly was trying hard not to laugh at Freddie's embarrassment. But Sam was cracking up as she turned toward him again.

Freddie turned the camera on himself. "*Ohhh, sooo* funny," he said sarcastically.

Sam grabbed the camera and dragged it back around so it was focused on her again.

"Freddie Benson, people," she told their viewers. "The most gullible boy in America!" Sam always enjoyed tormenting him!

"I'm usually not gullible," Freddie insisted.

Sam shook her head. "Dude, you're the easiest person to trick, ever."

"Untrue!" he argued.

"All right!" Carly announced, getting in the middle as usual. "I just wanna say, I feel really bad about tricking Freddie, which is why I'm giving him" — she pulled an envelope from her back pocket and held it up — "this one hundred dollar gift certificate to the Cheesecake Warehouse." She held the envelope out toward the camera — and Freddie.

"Seriously?" Freddie shifted the camera so he could take the envelope. He loved the Cheesecake Warehouse!

But Carly yanked the envelope back before he could get it. "Nope!" she declared. She turned to Sam and the two girls giggled. Then she opened the envelope and pulled out . . . a piece of lettuce? "It's just lettuce!"

"*Gotchaaaa!*" Sam declared, posing for the camera.

Carly laughed. "She made me do it!" she claimed again, pointing to Sam.

"Uh-huh!" Sam agreed, still laughing.

Carly waved the lettuce — a little too close to Sam's face. She gasped as her friend and co-host leaned over and took a bite out of it.

"Gimme that!" Sam insisted as Freddie cut away to their closing credits. She really would eat pretty much anything!

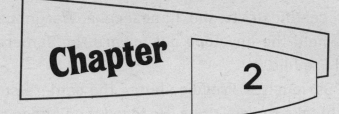
"**Y**ou're making too big a deal outta this," Carly told Sam the next day. They were at school and Sam was waiting impatiently as Carly gathered books from her locker.

"You don't understand," Sam insisted.

Carly shook her head. "I totally understand!"

Sam grabbed her by the shoulders. "Can I come stay at your house?" she begged.

"Sam, it's not that big of a deal," Carly replied, pulling free.

Just then Freddie walked over. Sam saw him first, and immediately swallowed whatever she'd been about to say. Carly turned and stared at Freddie as well, which made him suspicious.

"What were you guys talking about?" he asked.

"Ummm. . . ." Carly looked at Sam, who gave her a pleading look. "Nothin', just —"

"— the Middle East," Sam supplied.

Carly nodded. "Lotta tension there."

"Tough situation," Sam added.

She and Carly shared a glance. Then Carly slammed her locker shut and they hurried away.

"C'mon," Freddie called after them. "What were you guys talking about?"

They stopped, and Carly turned back, taking a few steps toward Freddie. She hated lying or keeping secrets from her friends. "Can't you just tell him?" she asked Sam.

But Sam was stubborn, as usual. "No!"

"He's gonna find out some time!" Carly pointed out.

Sam sighed. "Okay, fine, whatever." She turned to Freddie. "My sister's comin' home for a few days and I'm peeved off about it, okay?"

"It's just three days," Carly reminded her. "You can deal with it."

Freddie interrupted them. "Okay, wait a minute. Sam's sister?"

Sam said, "Yeah . . . Melanie." She looked disgusted just saying the name.

Freddie laughed and shook his head. "You don't have a sister."

"Yeah, she does," Carly confirmed.

Freddie made a silly face. "Well, then how come I've never heard of her?" he demanded.

Carly answered that one. "Cuz Sam hates to talk about her."

"She goes to a fancy boarding school, on a scholarship," Sam explained, "she gets perfect grades, never gets in trouble, always has clean hair — she makes me sick." It's true that those traits were the exact opposite of Sam, who was always getting detention, rarely paid attention in class, and tended to wash her hair by running in the rain.

"Aw, c'mon, she's sweet," Carly argued. Sam just rolled her eyes. Carly always wanted to see the best in everyone.

Freddie wasn't buying any of it, however. "Oh, will you guys just stop it?"

Both girls glanced at him. "What? What do you mean?" they asked together.

Freddie grinned at them triumphantly. "I'm not that gullible. I know Sam doesn't have a sister."

Sam glowered at him. "Yeah, I do."

"I've been to your house," he reminded her. "How come I've never seen a picture of this 'sister'?"

"You have," Sam replied. "You just didn't know it was Melanie cuz we look identical."

Carly nodded. "They're twins."

Freddie put on a big shocked expression. "Oh, *twiiiiins*," he repeated, hamming it up. Some student they didn't know walked by and Freddie turned to him. *"Twiiiiins!"* he exclaimed to the other kid, throwing his arms up in the air. Then he returned his attention to his friends. "*Riiiight*. Y'know, I have an uncle who's an avocado," he confided. "Yeah, we call him Uncle Green Mush."

Carly gave a little laugh, more at how ridiculous he was being than at his really dumb joke. "We're telling you the truth," she insisted.

Freddie shook his head. "I ain't fallin' for it."

"Who cares what he thinks?" Sam said finally, tapping Carly on the arm. "Let's go."

"People care what I think!" Freddie shouted after them as they walked off.

Mr. Howard was walking by right then. "No, they don't," he corrected. He didn't even stop.

Freddie sighed. "Yes, sir."

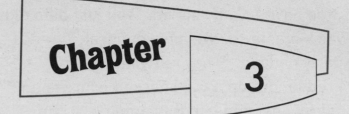

Chapter 3

Later, after school, Carly was studying at the kitchen table.

The apartment door opened, and her big brother, Spencer, came in. He had groceries.

"Look who's back," he called. "Me!"

Carly laughed as he set the bags on the kitchen counter. It was just the two of them. While their dad was stationed overseas, Spencer was Carly's guardian.

"How was the market?" she asked.

"*Kyoool*," Spencer answered. He reached into one bag and pulled out a package. "Your pork roast!" he announced, holding it out.

Carly stared at the plastic-wrapped meat. "Um," she said after a second, "I asked for an orange."

"You didn't say pork roast?"

She laughed. "No."

"Who was I talking to?" Spencer wondered out

loud as he turned away. "What kinda homework ya doin'?" he asked.

"I'm not," she replied. "I'm tutoring a kid who lives in our building."

Spencer smiled. "*Awww*, that's so nice of you."

"Well, his dad is paying me," Carly admitted.

Spencer nodded. "Good, cuz you owe me twenty-four bucks for the pork roast." He started mussing up Carly's hair, and she laughed, trying to pull away from him.

Just then a boy came downstairs from the bathroom. He was ten or eleven. "Hey," he told Carly as he entered the kitchen, "the soap in your bathroom smells awesome!"

Spencer glanced over, surprised. Then he saw who it was and screamed. *"AAAAAHHH!!!"*

Carly jumped up, startled. She was even more bewildered when he grabbed her chair and held it before him like a lion tamer!

The boy just stared at them like they'd both gone mad.

"Him?" Spencer demanded after a second. "You're tutoring . . . him?" He was still holding the chair in front of him.

"Yeah, that's Chuck," Carly answered.

"I know that's Chuck! Chuck is evil!" Spencer shouted. He waved the chair about.

"Spencer!" Carly took the chair away from him and set it back on the floor.

"He's my arch-nemesis!" Spencer insisted. "Once, he tried to hit me with a racquetball racquet, and then he smacked me around, and then another time he locked me in the basement and squirted me with a suspicious liquid!"

Carly was baffled. "Suspicious liquid?"

Chuck looked as confused as Carly felt. "I never did that stuff," he claimed.

Carly had had enough. She dragged Spencer around the kitchen island. "What's the matter with you?" she demanded.

Spencer set the bowl down. "You let my enemy penetrate my inner sanctum!" he complained.

"He's a nice kid," Carly insisted. He'd been great to tutor so far — polite, well behaved, and attentive. He was like Freddie in miniature.

But Spencer wasn't listening. "No — he's gonna do bad things to me," he insisted in a whine, pointing. Chuck was sitting at the kitchen table now, working on his math homework.

Carly shook her head. "You need to go take a hot bath or something," she suggested as she returned to the table herself.

"Bath?" Spencer muttered behind her.

"Sorry, Chuck," Carly said as she sat back down. "Where were we?"

Chuck gestured at the math problem he was working on. "Nine hundred divided by twelve."

Carly nodded. "Right. And the answer is . . . ?" She waited patiently.

Chuck wrote out the equation and did the math. "Seventy-five?"

Carly smiled. "Perfect!"

Chuck broke into a huge grin. "Yay, I'm learning!" he shouted.

"Okay," Carly told him, "let's check out your homework assignment for tomorrow." She leaned over to grab it from his backpack, which was sitting on the floor next to her.

Spencer had crossed around to the kitchen counter to get the rest of the groceries. He was facing into the kitchen, which meant he was looking directly at Chuck. The second Carly looked away, Chuck's whole expression changed. He went from being an innocent little boy to being a small demon as he scowled and glared at Spencer.

"You're dead," Chuck mouthed, pointing.

Spencer gasped. "Carly!" he shouted.

"What?" She glanced up. Spencer was pointing at Chuck — who was quietly doing his homework. Carly looked back and forth between them. Spencer let his hand drop.

"I'll put these away later," he muttered as he walked away.

Carly shook her head. She did love him, but sometimes her big brother was just plain weird.

She put that out of her head and went back to looking for Chuck's assignment sheet. She was kind of enjoying this whole tutoring thing!

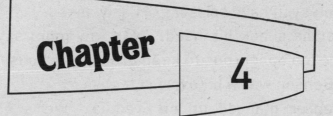

Chapter 4

That night, Carly and Spencer were sprawled on the couch, watching TV.

"The male elephant offers the female elephant a peanut," the narrator was explaining, describing the scene on TV.

Carly laughed. "What are we watching?"

Spencer glanced at her. "Elephant love," he answered.

Carly nodded. "Oh." That made sense.

Someone knocked on their door, and Carly took that as an opportunity to shut off the television.

The door swung open, and Freddie stepped inside. Not only was he one of her best friends, he was also their neighbor—he and his mom lived right across the hall. It made it easy to film *iCarly*, since they shot the Web show in the studio they'd put together upstairs!

"Hey," Freddie said. "Can I borrow scissors?"

"Don't you have scissors?" Carly asked.

Freddie shook his head. "Nah, my mom says they're too dangerous to keep around the house." Mrs. Benson was a bit overprotective.

Spencer glanced up at Freddie. "We've got scissors in the kitchen drawer." He gave Freddie a mock-stern look. "Can you handle 'em?"

Freddie put on an equally serious face. "I think I can."

"Come with me." Spencer levered himself up off the couch and led Freddie to the kitchen.

Just then the door intercom buzzed. Carly got up and hurried over to it.

"Yeah?" she said after pushing the TALK button.

"Carly, it's Melanie," the person downstairs replied. She really did sound just like Sam.

"Hey, Melanie! C'mon up." Carly buzzed her in.

"That Sam's sister?" Spencer asked from the kitchen.

Freddie rolled his eyes. "Oh, come on. They got you in on it, too?" He was sitting on one of the counter stools while Spencer searched for the scissors.

Spencer shook his head. "In on what?"

Freddie spun around to face Carly, who had walked over to join them. "Guys, I'm not fallin' for it. I know Sam doesn't have a twin sister."

"She does, too," Carly insisted.

The elevator dinged just then. The door slid up, and Melanie rushed out. She looked exactly like Sam, except that she was wearing cuter, more fashionable clothing and had her hair — her clean, well-tended hair — up in a ponytail.

"Hiiiii!" she squealed, running over to Carly and giving her a big hug.

Carly was just as excited. "Hey, Melanie!"

Freddie made a face. "Aw, gimme a break."

"Wow," Carly said after they separated, "I don't think I've seen you since"— she thought about it —"the seventh grade."

"I know!" Spencer had come around to the living room and now he tapped Melanie on the shoulder. She turned and gave him a big grin. "Hi, Spencer." Then she hugged him as well.

"Hey, kid," he replied.

Freddie couldn't believe it. "Okay, this is the stupidest thing ever," he announced.

77

Melanie looked at him, and her eyes widened. "Oh my gosh, you're Freddie." She smiled. "I recognize you from *iCarly.*"

"Oh, shut up!" Freddie told her.

For the first time since she'd arrived, Melanie's smile faltered. "Huh?" she said. "I'm confused."

"Really?" Freddie asked her. "Sam?"

Melanie paused and looked behind her, as if searching for someone else in the room.

"He thinks Sam's messin' with him about having a twin sister," Carly explained.

"*Ohhhhh!*" Melanie laughed. Even her laugh was different from Sam's — prettier and more ladylike. "I don't blame you," she assured Freddie. "It is the kinda thing Sam would do."

Freddie just made a face and stupid noises.

"Y'know, one time," Melanie told them, "she tried to convince me I was adopted?" She was still giggling at the thought.

Freddie nodded. He didn't look even the least bit convinced. "Uh-huh. And isn't it convenient that Sam isn't here right now?"

"She should be here." Melanie frowned and checked her watch. "It's almost eight."

Carly hopped off her stool. "Well, let's just go — I'll text Sam to meet us at the movie."

Melanie nodded, her blond ponytail bouncing. "Perfect!"

She followed Carly back over to the elevator.

"Wonderful," Freddie told them both, clapping slowly. "Bravo! Very believable performance, Carly and Sam." He put emphasis on the "Sam."

The elevator opened, and the two girls stepped into it. "Freddie — I'm really Melanie," Melanie told him.

"D'uh-huh," he responded, making his stupid face again.

Carly laughed at him. "Later."

"Nice meeting you," Melanie called out.

"Uh, okay," Freddie mocked. The elevator shut and he returned to the kitchen counter. "How can they think I'm that gullible?" he asked Spencer, who handed him a pair of scissors.

Spencer looked at him. "Clown Day?" he asked.

Freddie grimaced. "That email looked really real!"

Spencer waved it off. "Don't feel bad. When I

was a kid at sleepaway camp, my friends tricked me into thinking it was Naked Day." He paused, and a pained look appeared on his face. "You ever play dodgeball naked?"

Freddie shook his head slowly. "No."

"Don't ever do it," Spencer warned.

"I won't."

Spencer sighed. He looked like he was reliving the moment.

Freddie turned and made his way toward the door without another word. Behind him, Spencer headed to his room.

Neither of them saw the cabinet under the kitchen sink open — or Chuck emerge and glance around. He was wearing a small tool belt. He had an evil expression on his face as he pulled out a screwdriver and stepped over to inspect one of the kitchen cabinets.

Freddie was just crossing the hall to his apartment when Sam stepped around the corner.

"Hey, dish rag," she said.

Freddie stopped and turned around to study her. Sam was wearing the same outfit she had on at school today. Her hair, as usual, was long and loose and all over the place.

"Impressive," Freddie admitted. "What, you changed your clothes and hair in the lobby, then took the main elevator back up here?"

"What are you yappin' on about now?" Sam snarled. Then her pocket chirped. "Wait." She extracted her cell phone and read the new text message she'd just received. "Ah, I gotta go meet Carly and Melanie at the Omniplex."

Freddie grinned. "*Okaaaay*, well, better hurry—you don't wanna keep yourself waiting." Sam just shook her head and headed toward the elevator, texting Carly as she went.

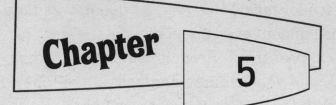

Chapter 5

The next day after school, Carly and Sam were sitting at their favorite hangout, the Groovy Smoothie. They each had a smoothie, of course, and there was a third one on the table in front of them. Sam had an order of fries as well.

Carly was busy telling Sam about the latest incident at their apartment. "So I come running downstairs," she told her friend, "and Spencer is standing there in his pajamas."

"Ugh," Sam responded, slurping her smoothie.

"I know. Anyway, he's covered in some kind of black goop. It's all over his face, his hair, his shirt — everywhere!"

"Yuck!" Then Sam paused. "What did it taste like?"

Carly stared at her. "I don't know! I didn't even want to touch it, let alone taste it!"

Sam grinned at her. "Did Spencer taste it?"

Carly sighed. "Yes. He said it was disgusting." She shook her head. "Anyway, he claimed Chuck did that to him!"

"Who, that sweet little kid you're tutoring?" Sam scoffed.

"Exactly! He said Chuck had some kind of pump-gun thing, and squirted him with it, then took off before I came downstairs." Carly frowned. "This whole imagined feud with Chuck is getting way out of hand."

"Your brother's gone cuckoo," Sam declared, waving her finger in circles at her head.

"Maybe." Carly laughed. "You know the cupboard doors and the fridge door all came off their hinges yesterday? He blamed that one on Chuck, too!"

"Unreal!"

They were both still chuckling when Freddie joined them. "Hey." He sank into the chair across from them.

"Oh, hi," Carly replied. From Sam he got "Fred-a-cheenie." It was a Sam thing; Freddie had long since stopped trying to figure it out.

"So," he asked her instead, "are you Sam right

83

now or Melanie?" He made air quotes around the second name.

Sam shrugged. "I dunno, does this hurt?" Then she punched him in the arm. Hard.

That was also a Sam thing: violence. Especially where Freddie was concerned.

"Ow!" He rubbed at his arm. "Yeah, it hurt!"

Now Sam broke into a grin. "Then I'm Sam."

In retaliation, Freddie took one of her fries. "I thought you had detention today," he said.

"I do." That was no real surprise — it seemed like Sam had detention almost every day. Freddie was pretty sure she spent more time in detention than she did in actual class.

"She snuck out," Carly explained.

That surprised him. "Won't Miss Briggs know you ditched?" Miss Briggs was in charge of detention, and she was not a lady Freddie would want mad at him. Of course, he didn't want anybody mad at him.

Sam, however, seemed unconcerned. "Nah, she only comes for the first five minutes, then she leaves to go make out with Mr. Howard in the teachers' lounge."

Carly shuddered. "Ulch. People over thirty really should not make out."

Sam and Freddie both agreed that was horribly wrong.

Then Freddie noticed the third drink. "Whose smoothie?" he asked. Carly could tell by his tone that he was hoping it was for him.

But no. "Melanie's," Sam answered.

"Oh." He grinned and reached across the table to snatch it up. "So this is Melanie's smoothie? Then where is 'Mythical Melanie'?" Freddie exaggerated the name to show how little he believed them.

Sam just rolled her eyes and gestured behind her. "In the bathroom."

"Even twins have to go sometimes," Carly added.

Freddie was going to say something snarky about always going in pairs when Sam's cell phone rang.

"Yeah, what's up?" she answered.

Freddie ignored her and turned back to Carly. "Then maybe I'll just wait here til 'Melanie' comes out of the bathroom," he offered.

"Aw, man!" Sam's exclamation made them both glance at her, however. She looked angry—and slightly panicked.

"What's wrong?" Carly inquired.

Sam pulled the phone away long enough to answer her. "Briggs came back to detention and saw I ditched." She switched her attention back to the phone. "Uh, just tell her I had to puke! I'll be back there in five minutes!" She hung up and stood quickly, grabbing her backpack from beside her chair.

"Don'tcha have to wait for 'Melanie'?" Freddie asked smugly. He was still holding the third smoothie.

Sam shrugged. "Tell her I'll meet her later at home."

"Wait," Carly called out as Sam started to leave, "you didn't pay for your smoothie."

"I didn't finish it!" Sam shouted back over her shoulder. Then she ran out.

Carly sighed. Then she grabbed Sam's smoothie off the table and hefted it.

She made a face at Freddie. "She did finish

it." Which didn't really surprise either of them. When did Sam ever not finish her food?

Just then a salesman stopped by their table. He was tall and skinny, and his long dark hair spilled out from under his bright kerchief. Big gold hoops dangled from his ears. He was carrying a long stick with pickles impaled upon it. "Would the gentleman care for a pickle?" he asked Freddie.

Freddie looked a little bewildered. "Uh, no, I don't wanna pickle."

The salesman didn't look very happy with that answer. "Why—you afraid of pickles? Scared to take a walk on the pickle side a' town?" He seemed to be taking Freddie's refusal very personally.

"No," Freddie told him, frowning. "I just think that pickles and smoothies don't really go together."

Now the guy was getting angry. "Oh!" he snapped. "Well, pardon me for thinkin' that all foods and beverages could get along!"

The pickle salesman stomped off just as Melanie approached. She was wearing a cute pink sweater, designer jeans, and a string of pearls.

"Hey, Freddie!" She gave him a big, bright smile. It dimmed a little as she glanced around and realized it was just Freddie and Carly. "Where's Sam?"

Carly explained, "She had to go back to detention."

"Yes," Freddie agreed. "And isn't it interesting how 'Sam' had to leave — right before you showed up here?"

Melanie laughed as she sat next to Carly. "Is he still on this?"

Carly rolled her eyes. "Uh-huh."

"I will say," Freddie told "Melanie," "it's impressive that you changed your clothes and hair so fast."

Melanie sighed. "Freddie, I'm really Melanie. I'm really Sam's sister." She sounded sincere.

But Freddie wasn't buying it. "Oh, are you?" He slapped his hands to his face in mock amazement.

"I am." She stood and reached into her purse, then pulled out some money and set it down on the table. "Anyway, I gotta go meet my mom at the clinic."

Melanie turned to go, but Freddie called out,

"Wait!" He looked like he was up to something.

She turned back as Freddie got up and walked over to her. "Since you're 'Melanie,'" he announced, making a big deal out of her name as always, "how would you like to go on a date with me this Saturday night?" He was smirking as he asked.

Melanie glanced at Carly, surprised. So was Carly! "Oh." Then Melanie smiled. "Well, that'd be really cool. I'd love to!" Her smile was even brighter now.

Freddie nodded, not really hearing what she'd said. "Oh, you—" Her answer sank in, and he stared at her. "Really?"

She nodded. "Sure."

"Okay, then," Freddie said, recovering from his shock. He still looked a bit unsure, though.

Her responding smile was wide and cheerful. "Okay. Bye."

Melanie walked out, and after a second Freddie sat back down across from Carly.

"Wow," she said once he was seated, "that came outta nowhere." She wasn't entirely sure how she felt about it, either. Freddie had been chasing after her since they'd first met. Now he'd

known Melanie less than a day and he was asking her out? But Freddie seemed pleased with himself. "Yep," he answered. "Cuz I'm a genius."

Now Carly was even more puzzled. "Huh?"

Freddie leaned forward. "Sam would rather chew broken glass than go on a date with me for a whole Saturday night," he confided. He raised the discarded smoothie. "No way she's gonna go through with this."

Carly shook her head. "You asked Melanie," she pointed out.

He just laughed. "*Okaaaay.* You can pretend I'm goin' on a date with Melanie, but I know I've got a date with Sam."

He took a triumphant sip of Melanie's smoothie — but then looked horrified and coughed, spitting it back up.

Carly reared back. "What's wrong?" she asked.

Freddie glanced over at her. He looked completely panicked. "I've got a date with Sam!" he choked out.

Suddenly, the pickle salesman was leaning in over Freddie's shoulder. "Wanna buy a pickle?"

Freddie glared at the man. "NO!!!!!"

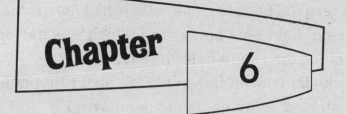

Chapter 6

"Uhhh . . ." Chuck muttered. He and Carly were sitting on the living room couch together, going over his math again. The poor kid did have trouble solving equations, but he was getting better with Carly's help.

"Next I—" he started now, reaching the next part of the homework problem. He trailed off, unsure what to do next.

"Subtract twenty-six from seven hundred," Carly prompted him. He nodded and scribbled that down on the next line, then worked out the answer before moving to the next step.

There was a knock at the door, and Freddie entered. He was holding two sweaters.

"Hey," he said.

"Tutoring," Carly reminded him.

"This'll just take a sec," he assured her. He held the sweaters up. One was a dark blue-and-

black argyle pattern. The other had horizontal stripes of light blue and gray. "Which sweater do you think Sam would hate the most?"

Carly didn't even have to think about that one. "The stripes." Sam hated stripes! "Why?"

Freddie grinned. "Then I'm wearin' the stripes on my date with her."

Carly sighed and leaned forward. "You're going out with Melanie — not Sam," she reminded him yet again. But that just made Freddie roll his eyes for the thousandth time.

Chuck smiled at her. "Hey, when I get older," he said softly, "maybe I could go on a date with you."

Awww, that was so sweet! Carly beamed at him, which only made the kid smile even more. "*Ohhhh*, Chuck," she told him, giggling. She'd never had a little kid crush on her like that before!

Big kids, however, were a different matter. As she remembered all too well when Freddie leaned in and advised, "Don't waste your time, kid. I've been barkin' up that tree since sixth grade."

Carly laughed at him as well, and Freddie left without saying good-bye. He was acting so weird lately!

She didn't have time to worry about that right now, though. First she needed to finish tutoring Chuck. Then —

Her thoughts scattered as a loud *"Awwwww!!"* echoed through the apartment.

That sounded like Spencer!

"What happened?" Carly called.

A second later her brother emerged from the upstairs. He was holding his motorcycle helmet in one hand, cradled like a basket. His other hand was inside the helmet!

"You wanna know what happened?" he demanded as he stomped toward them. "That little pimple filled my motorcycle helmet with chunky red goo!"

Spencer pulled his hand out of the helmet — and showed off the disgusting, thick red slime that coated it. It was like someone had mixed red Jell-O with red paint and filled the helmet with the vile concoction.

"Ewwwww!" Carly got up and stepped over to get a better look, though she carefully kept out of arm's reach. "What is that?!"

Spencer grimaced. "I wish I knew!"

He studied the goop as it dripped off his hand. It was so red! So . . . inviting! So . . . tasty? He brought his hand toward his mouth, slowly, and leaned in —

"Don't taste it!" Carly shouted.

"Right!" He jerked his hand away and straightened up. Then he glared at the goop. "It's so gross!" He set the helmet on the kitchen counter. Upside-down, fortunately.

Chuck had gotten up to see, as well. "Want me to get you a paper towel?" he offered. He sounded so . . . nice.

Carly certainly thought so. *"Awww!"* She smiled at the boy.

But Spencer wasn't falling for it. "Don't go *'Awww!'*" he insisted. "He did this!" Spencer pointed with his goo-covered hand.

"I did not!" Chuck protested. But Carly didn't see the way the boy glared at Spencer when she wasn't looking.

Instead she defended Chuck. "Stop picking on him!" she insisted. "Just use your other helmet."

Spencer was busy wiping the goo off his hand with a dish towel. "You and Sam took my

94

other helmet to use for some *iCarly* thing," he reminded her.

Oh. Right. "Then I'll go get it," Carly promised. She headed for the stairs, but paused to tell her brother, "You need to calm down and take a bubble bath or something."

"Y'know, bathing isn't the answer to everything," Spencer called after her.

Now Spencer was alone with Chuck. He tossed the dish towel onto the counter and glared at the boy. Chuck had returned to the couch and his homework — at least, that's what he was pretending. But Spencer wasn't falling for it.

"Alright, Chuck — now you listen to me." The boy set his homework aside and turned, an ugly sneer across his face. Spencer stalked over to the couch and leaned in close, trying his best to look menacing. "I know what you are. You may have Carly fooled, but I know exactly wh —"

That was when Chuck took action! He reached out and grabbed Spencer's hand, which had been pointing at him accusingly, and wrapped his other arm around Spencer's neck. Then he twisted forward and yanked down hard.

"*Yaahhh!*" Spencer went flying over the couch and smacked hard onto the top of the coffee table!

Somehow Chuck'd held onto Spencer's throat, and now the boy leaped to his feet. He transferred his hold to Spencer's shirt and dragged him around until he was stretched out across the coffee table.

Then the boy began wailing on him!

Slap! Slap! Slap! Chuck's free hand was a blur as it slammed back and forth across Spencer's face. Spencer tried to defend himself, but it was no use. The little kid was just too strong for him!

He was saved by the sound of footsteps from above. Chuck shoved Spencer off the coffee table, on the far side from the couch. While Spencer was trying to shake off the blows, Chuck dropped back onto the couch and reached for his math notebook again. By the time Carly emerged from the upstairs, Spencer's old motorcycle helmet in her hands, Chuck was quietly doing his homework as if nothing had happened. Spencer, however, was still stretched out on the ground, groaning.

"Here's your other helm —" Carly started, but

trailed off as she took in the scene before her. "Why are you on the floor?"

Chuck looked up as if seeing Spencer for the first time. "Maybe he had a stroke," the boy suggested.

Spencer hauled himself to his feet. Then he reached out and grabbed Carly by the arm.

"Come with me."

"I'm not done tutoring!" Carly protested as her brother began to drag her back toward the stairs.

"This'll just take a second," he assured her.

"Spencer!"

"Don't protest!" he demanded.

"Where are we going?" she asked, finally giving in and letting him lead her away.

But he refused to say. "Just come on!"

Carly had no choice but to leave Chuck behind and go along with whatever Spencer wanted.

She hoped Chuck would be all right downstairs by himself.

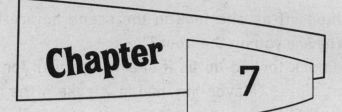

Chapter 7

Spencer led Carly upstairs, to the hall outside the *iCarly* studio. He shut the door to the stairs behind them.

"I have to finish my tutoring session with Chuck," Carly reminded him, pulling her arm free. But Spencer ignored her plea. Instead he knelt by the bench and grabbed something sitting on the floor beside it. When he stood up, he had a small laptop in his hands.

"*Shhhhhhh,*" he told her, silencing her complaints. "Look at this."

Carly frowned. "Whose laptop is that?" It didn't look at all familiar.

"Socko's," her brother answered. That made sense. Socko was one of Spencer's best friends. He had all kinds of crazy gadgets, and sometimes let Spencer borrow them. "He lent it to me with some special software and a couple of teeny little

secret video cameras." Spencer was fiddling with the computer, tapping in commands and opening some sort of program.

"Okay," Carly started. "I really don't have time to—"

Spencer held out a hand to stop her. "Watch this." He turned the laptop so the screen was facing her. "Take a look at what happened downstairs two minutes ago." Sure enough, the screen showed their living room! Chuck was sitting on the sofa doing his homework, and Carly thought she saw her own foot on the stairs at the top of the image. This must have been right when she came up here to look for Spencer's helmet!

"I don't want to!" she protested. She didn't have time for his crazy stories about Chuck right now!

"Just look at it!" Spencer insisted.

"Okay!" Just to humor him, Carly watched the laptop screen as Spencer hit PLAY—

—and then she stared, amazed.

She saw Spencer lean across the couch, trying to bully Chuck—and saw Chuck grab him, flip him over onto the coffee table, and start beating him!

Carly couldn't believe it. "That lying little

beast!" she declared. He'd been lying to her the whole time!

"Y'see?" Spencer closed the Pearbook. "He grabbed me, pulled me over the couch, and then wailed on me!" He set the laptop on the bench so he could act out part of the attack.

"I know!" Carly still couldn't believe it. Chuck—sweet little Chuck—had beaten up her big brother! "You gotta start working out!" she told Spencer.

He stared at her. "That's not the point!" he insisted. "Now you know I was right! He's evil!" A gleam came to Spencer's eye. "And I want revenge!"

He turned to go, but Carly grabbed his arm, stopping him.

"No," she said. Oh, she understood Spencer's desire for revenge. Chuck had played her, too. And that totally demanded payback! But Spencer would storm down there and stick the boy into a trashcan or something. She loved her brother, but he wasn't very subtle. No, this called for something more devious.

Sam would have been good for a half dozen

ideas. But Carly was no slouch when it came to being devious.

She thought for a second. Then she had it. She knew Chuck's weakness — and exactly how to exploit it.

"I know how to get him back. Trust me."

Her brother didn't even hesitate. "Okay," he agreed. That was why she loved him. He always had her back — and he knew she had his.

Carly smiled. She was still holding him by the arm, and she squeezed it. Then she squeezed a little higher. "You do have to start working out," she insisted. It was like holding onto a wet noodle!

Spencer yanked his arm free. "Stop squishing it!" He opened the door and headed back downstairs. Carly followed. She couldn't resist grabbing at his arm a few more times, though.

Spencer headed for his room — Carly had warned him that it'd work better if he was nowhere around when she sprang her trap for Chuck, and he had agreed. So she continued down to the living room by herself.

Chuck was still sitting on the couch, right where she'd left him. She paused on the landing for a second. He seemed so innocent from here! But she'd seen the video footage. She knew he was really a little monster.

This was going to be tough to pull off.

"Hey, Chuck," she called out as she took the last few stairs. "Sorry to keep you waiting." She forced herself to smile pleasantly at him, and even to giggle a little bit.

"Oh, it's okay," he assured her. "I drew you a flower." He held up his notebook. He'd drawn a large daisy in pencil. It wasn't half-bad.

If she hadn't known better, she would have thought he was really sweet. Now the notion made her stomach turn.

But she pretended differently. "*Awww.* You're so sweet," she told him as she came around the couch. He beamed at her, and she forced herself to beam right back. Then she got down to business. "Anyway, since you've got your big test on Monday, we should go over the new international math laws that were just passed by the U.N."

Chuck looked surprised. And more than a little

concerned. Good. "International math laws?" he asked.

Carly sank down on the couch next to him. "Uh-huh. They made some changes, so we gotta make sure you understand all the new rules."

Now he looked terrified. Perfect.

Carly leaned in toward him and lowered her voice like she was sharing a secret. "Now, the biggest news is that they've created a new number." She acted all excited.

"A new number?" He still looked confused, but he wasn't arguing. He was falling for it!

Carly said, "Yep — between five and six. It's called derf." She made the name up on the spot.

Chuck repeated it dutifully. "Derf."

"Right. And it looks like this." Carly took the notebook from him, turned to a blank page, and drew a strange symbol on it. "That's a derf. See?" The symbol looked a lot like an "and" sign. Probably because it was one. Or near enough. She was counting on his not knowing that.

Chuck studied the image. "Oh."

Carly smiled. "So, now it goes: one, two, three, four, five, derf, six, seven. Got it?"

He nodded. "I think so." He was definitely taking this seriously! But then, he had no reason to think Carly would lie to him. Especially about something like this.

"Good." Carly laid the notebook in her lap. "And so then it goes: thirteen, fourteen, fifteen . . . and what's next?" She looked at him expectantly.

Chuck thought for a second before finally venturing, "Derfteen?"

Carly smiled. "Wow! You catch on fast."

Chuck smiled. "Thanks."

She wasn't sure she could keep a straight face if she looked at him, so she turned to a fresh page in the notebook and wrote out a math problem, explaining it as she went. "So, if we take twelve, and multiply that by eighty-one, and then divide by two, we get . . . ?"

Chuck took the notebook from her, read it, and worked out the rest of the answer. "Four hundred and derfty-seven?"

Carly tried to keep from smirking as she agreed. "Awesome!"

Chuck looked pleased with himself.

That would change soon enough.

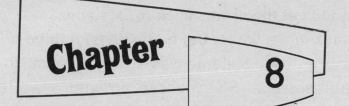

Chapter 8

The scene at Quisp was wild that night. The teen dance club was pulsing with a loud techno dance beat, and there were kids dancing and swaying and grooving everywhere.

Freddie was at the beverage station, where he'd just gotten two tall, fruity drinks. One for him — and one for "Melanie."

Now he just had to get back across the dance floor, to where she waited on one of the cushy couches strewn around the room.

But it wasn't that easy. Several girls bumped into him. Then two of them cornered Freddie between them and started dancing with him, writhing around him to the heavy beat.

Under other circumstances, Freddie would have really enjoyed that. Both girls were super-hot, after all.

But right now he was a man on a mission.

He had to get the drinks back to "Melanie."

It took him a while, but he finally stumbled off the dance floor. Melanie was sitting on a couch, texting someone. She glanced up with a smile when Freddie joined her and set the glasses down on the blue-lit glass table.

"Here we go," he told her.

Melanie looked at them and laughed. "Get thirsty on the way here?" The glasses were completely empty—being body-slammed by those two girls had made Freddie spill their contents all over the dance floor.

He hoped nobody slipped on the puddles.

"Sort of," he replied. He didn't want to admit what had happened. Instead he glanced over at his "date." "So, 'Melanie,'" he told her. "You look pretty hot tonight."

She did, too. She was wearing a sleeveless red dress with a ruffled neck, and over that she had on a long strand of pearls. She'd braided her hair a bit more elaborately—and was that makeup she was wearing? Sam hated makeup!

She gave him a huge smile. "Thanks. I love your shirt."

Freddie shook his head. "No, you don't," he argued. "Carly said you hate stripes."

Melanie sighed. "Sam hates stripes."

"How long are you gonna keep this up?" Freddie asked her. He shoved her arm. "Just admit you're Sam and we can leave."

"I would — *ow* — but I'm not Sam," Melanie told him. She rubbed at her arm. She looked disappointed and a little hurt.

Freddie had never realized what a good actress Sam could be.

He wasn't going to break her. Not just by asking, or by putting her in an awkward situation.

He'd have to do something a bit more drastic.

"Okay." He sidled closer to her on the couch. "If you're not Sam, then I guess you wouldn't mind if I held your hand." He took her hand in his and held it gently, like they were on a real date and he really liked her.

Like it was Carly's hand he was holding.

"I don't mind at all," Melanie replied. Her smile this time was a little more embarrassed. "I think you're really cute," she admitted softly.

Freddie couldn't believe what he was hearing.

"How can you say that without vomiting?"

"What?" Now she looked really confused. And upset. For a second, Freddie wondered if . . . but no. He knew better. He wasn't going to fall for her act, no matter how convincing she was.

Then he noticed that the music had changed. The techno beat had been replaced by a smoother, more romantic rhythm. Freddie smiled.

"All right. If you're not Sam, I suppose you wouldn't mind dancing — with me." He gave her a sly look. That was sure to work.

But Melanie smiled and stood up. "I'd love to."

Freddie stared at her. "This is a slow dance, y'know."

She nodded. "I know."

"We'll have to dance together," he clarified. "Pressed against each other."

"Yeah," she agreed. "Let's go."

She took his hand and led him out onto the dance floor. Freddie couldn't believe it. He put her arms around her waist but kept them loose so there was still some space between them.

Apparently that wasn't good enough for Melanie, though. She tugged him closer and

wrapped her arms around his neck. Then they started swaying to the music.

Finally, Freddie couldn't stand it any longer. "I can't believe you're doing this," he told her.

Melanie laughed at his expression. "Why? I like you," she insisted.

Freddie scowled at her. "You hate me — you always have."

"Maybe Sam hates you." She shrugged.

"You are Sam!"

Melanie gave him a little smirk. "Really? Would Sam do this?" Then she leaned in — and kissed him! Right on the mouth!

Freddie was so surprised he didn't even pull away for several seconds. Besides, it was nice.

He shook himself and reared back, staring at her. He knew his mouth was hanging open, but he couldn't help it.

Melanie just waited, a tiny grin on her face, watching his reaction.

Finally Freddie found his voice again. "You swore we'd never do that again!" he whispered. A while back, he and Sam had decided that, since neither of them had ever kissed anyone before,

they should kiss each other. Just to get the whole "first kiss" thing over with. They'd sworn they'd never tell anyone about it, and that they'd go right back to hating each other afterward.

Melanie looked a little surprised by that one, but then she grinned. "I didn't swear anything," she pointed out. And she leaned in to kiss him again.

Freddie wasn't going to get taken by surprise a second time! He pulled free from her and took a step back. Melanie followed. She wasn't backing off! Freddie had no choice.

He ran.

And Melanie, laughing, chased after him. The two of them zigzagged all over the dance floor, Freddie in a panic and Melanie giggling.

All in all, it was one of Freddie's better dates.

Chapter 9

Monday afternoon after school, Carly and Sam were chilling out at Carly's loft. They were sitting at either ends of the living room couch, each of them holding a tennis racquet. Sam had blown up a purple balloon, and they were batting it back and forth between them.

"Y'know what's a stupid letter?" Sam asked.

Carly nodded and knocked the balloon to her friend. "Q?"

Sam nodded. "Yeah. Why do I hate Q so much?" She stretched to swat the balloon back over.

"Cuz it's so obviously just an O," Carly answered, "tryin' to be all fancy with its pointless little tail."

Sam leaned back to go for the balloon as it floated behind the couch. "Ulch. Q's pathetic."

A knock at the door interrupted their game.

"Hey," Spencer asked, "could one a' you guys get that? I'm sculpturing." He was standing on a ladder in the kitchen, wiring something up along the support column there. Spencer's art was actually pretty cool, or at least it was always interesting. Other people apparently thought so, too, since that was how he made his living. And paid for their apartment, groceries, and everything else.

"Sure." Carly set her racquet down on the couch and hopped up to get the door.

She pulled it open — to reveal a large, annoyed-looking dark-haired man and a small, sullen boy.

"Oh." Carly backed up a few paces to let them enter. "Hi, Mr. Chambers," she greeted the man. Then she glared at his son. "Chuck."

Sam watched them from the couch, and sneered in disgust. "Ugh. Stripes." Mr. Chambers was wearing a striped rugby shirt.

"Carly," Chuck's dad began, "I just wanted to let you know we're not going to continue with the tutoring. Chuck failed his math test." He kept one hand firmly on Chuck's shoulder, as if to keep him from bolting.

Carly did her best to look completely shocked. "Oh, no!"

"It's not your fault," Mr. Chambers assured her. "He made up some fake number called 'derf.'"

Now she acted surprised and confused. "Derf?" she repeated.

Chuck couldn't take it anymore. "I learned it from you!" he wailed at her.

Carly glanced at Chuck's dad and shook her head, shrugging slightly like she had no idea what Chuck was talking about.

"Okay, that does it, Chuck," Mr. Chambers told his son. "If you're gonna blame Carly for your failure, then I'm grounding you for three weeks."

Chuck looked like he was about to cry. *"Daaaad!!!"*

Just then Spencer walked over to join them. "Mr. Chambers," he began seriously, "y'know, I also had trouble with math when I was a boy. So my dad sent me to math camp for the whole summer." Carly nodded beside him, confirming his tale.

Mr. Chambers looked interested. "Math camp?" he repeated slowly.

Chuck, however, was furious. "Math camp?"

"Yes." Spencer smiled and reached into his

back pocket. "Here's a brochure." He handed it to Mr. Chambers and gave Chuck a knowing look. Chuck glared back at him.

"Oooh," Mr. Chambers said, reading the brochure. "'Camp Addemup.' This looks perfect!"

Spencer smiled down at the boy who had so often made his life completely miserable. "Enjoy your summer, Chuck."

Carly leaned in. "Yeah . . . Chuck."

"Let's go, son," Mr. Chambers told Chuck. Chuck glared at Carly and Spencer but there was nothing he could do with his dad there. The two of them walked out.

Spencer and Carly shut the door behind the pair. Then they high-fived. Nobody messed with Carly and her brother and got away with it!

"Yes!" Spencer shouted. "That was fun. I'm gonna go take a victory bath." He bounded up the stairs toward his room.

"Shave your toes!" Carly shouted after him.

Spencer's voice carried back to her in a whine. *"Nooooo!"*

Carly returned to the couch and reclaimed her racquet. "So where were we?" she asked. Sam

was bouncing the balloon on her racquet, and batted it back over to Carly.

"Hittin' a balloon," Sam answered with a laugh. "Hatin' Q."

Carly nodded. "Right." She hit the balloon back.

She heard a knock on the front door, but it opened before she could even get up to answer it, and Freddie walked in.

"Hey. Here's your—" he started, holding out the pair of scissors, but he stopped when he spotted Sam. "Oh. You're here."

Sam snorted. "Yeah, like seein' your face freshens up my day."

"You sure seemed to like my face last night," Freddie retorted after setting the scissors on the kitchen counter. "When you had your lips all over it!"

Sam set aside her racquet and rose from the couch. "That wasn't me, dipthong."

Carly got up as well. "You and Melanie kissed?" She was shocked. And maybe even a little hurt. Asking Melanie out to prove a point was one thing. Kissing her was something altogether different!

"Man!" Freddie burst out. "How long are you two gonna keep tryin' to trick me with the whole 'Melanie' thing? I told you, I'm not that gullible!" He raised his voice. "I know there's no Melanie!"

Carly upped her volume as well. "Yes there —"

She didn't finish her statement — because Sam interrupted her. "Whoa!" She glanced at Carly and shrugged. "Let's just stop," Sam suggested. "It didn't work."

Carly stared at her. "It didn't?"

Sam swiveled back toward Freddie and took a few lazy steps toward him. "Okay," she said slowly. "You won. We tried to trick you, but we couldn't pull it off." She glanced back at Carly, who was frowning at her.

Freddie, on the other hand, looked delighted. "Ha! Then admit there's no Melanie, and that I'm not gullible, and that I'm too smart for you."

"There's no Melanie," Sam repeated in almost a singsong voice, "you're not gullible . . . and you're too smart for me."

"That's right!" Freddie laughed at her. "In your face, Puckett!" Then he turned and sauntered past them toward the door. "Bye, ladies."

Carly watched Freddie go. "He loves to be right," she said after he'd shut the door behind him.

Sam nodded. "All boys do."

"Totally."

They had just turned back toward the couch when the elevator dinged. A second later, as Sam and Carly were gathering their coats, the elevator door slid up —

— and Melanie stepped out.

"Hey!" she called out. "We goin' to the mall?"

"Yep, let's hit it," Carly and Sam agreed. They both shrugged into their jackets, Carly grabbed her purse, and they joined Melanie in the elevator.

The door hadn't even closed yet when Sam shook her head. "How could you make out with Freddie?" she demanded.

Her sister laughed. "He's adorable!" she pointed out. She was practically gushing.

Carly shook her head. "I can't believe you two are sisters," she admitted.

Sam and Melanie both shrugged. "Me, either," they said in unison.

The elevator door closed behind them.

Read all about the hottest show on the web!

Carly and Sam have been best friends for years. But on the fifth anniversary of their friendship, they get into a big fight. Will they work it out?

Carly and Sam are hatching chicks for a school project. But when the chicks get lost things get a little out of control!

Look for these and other iCarly books wherever books are sold.

SCHOLASTIC and associated logos are trademarks and/or registered trademarks of Scholastic Inc. © 2010 Viacom International Inc. All Rights Reserved. Nickelodeon, iCarly and all related titles and logos are trademarks of Viacom International Inc.

www.scholastic.com
www.icarly.com

ICARLYF10